A Note to Parents

DK READERS is a compelling program for beginning readers, designed in conjunction with leading literacy experts, including Dr. Linda Gambrell, Professor of Education at Clemson University. Dr. Gambrell has served as President of the National Reading Conference, the College Reading Association, and the International Reading Association.

The DK ReaderActives line provides action-oriented illustrations, colorful page designs, and stories in which children get to make their own choices. Multiple story paths encourage children to reread their adventures to explore every possible ending. Each DK ReaderActive is guaranteed to capture a child's interest while developing his or her reading skills, general knowledge, and love of reading.

Unlike DK READERS, DK ReaderActives are not assigned a specific reading level. Generally, DK ReaderActives are best suited to Levels 2 and 3 in the list below. Younger children will surely enjoy making the story's choices while adults read aloud to them. Likewise, older children will appreciate picking their own path and trying new options with each reading.

> **Pre-level 1:** Learning to read
>
> **Level 1:** Beginning to read
>
> **Level 2:** Beginning to read alone
>
> **Level 3:** Reading alone
>
> **Level 4:** Proficient readers

The "normal" age at which a child begins to read can be anywhere from three to eight years old. Adult participation through the lower levels is very helpful for providing encouragement, discussing storylines, and sounding out unfamiliar words. No matter which ReaderActive title you select, you can be sure that you are helping your child learn to read interactively!

LONDON, NEW YORK, MUNICH,
MELBOURNE, and DELHI

For DK/BradyGames

Global Strategy Guide Publisher
Mike Degler

Licensing Manager
Christian Sumner

Editor-In-Chief
H. Leigh Davis

Marketing Manager
Katie Hemlock

Digital Publishing Manager
Tim Cox

Operations Manager
Stacey Beheler

Title Manager
Tim Fitzpatrick

Book Designer
Tim Amrhein

Production Designer
Wil Cruz

Reading Consultant
Linda B. Gambrell, Ph.D.

DK/BradyGAMES
800 East 96th St., 3rd floor
Indianapolis, IN 46240

12 13 14   10 9 8 7 6 5 4 3 2 1

A catalog record for this book is available from the Library of Congress.

ISBN: 978-1-4654-0393-3 (Paperback)

Printed and bound by Lake Book Manufacturing, Inc.

Discover more at
www.dk.com

Adventures in the Wild!

Written by Simcha Whitehill

DK Publishing

FX: 6-13

HOW TO USE THIS READERACTIVE

Welcome to this Pokémon ReaderActive, where *you* decide how the story unfolds! As you read, you'll find instructions at the bottom of each section of the story. These instructions fall into three categories:

1. Some instructions tell you to skip to a certain page—they look like this:

> Continue to **page 58**.

When you see an instruction like this, simply turn to the page that's listed and continue reading.

2. Other instructions let you make a choice. This is how you decide where the story takes you! Each of your options is described in its own bar, like this:

> To act fast and choose Stunfisk to step in and battle Litwick, proceed to **page 26, bottom**.

> To have Dewott hose down the fire, proceed to **page 57, bottom**.

Whichever option you choose, just skip to the listed page and continue reading. In the example above, let's say you decide to choose the first option. In that case, just turn to **PAGE 26**. Notice that the instruction also tells you to read the **BOTTOM** entry. Sometimes instructions tell you to read the **TOP** or the **BOTTOM** of a certain page. Pay attention to this—when you turn to such a page, you'll see that the entries are marked with the words "TOP" and "BOTTOM," like this:

> **TOP**   **BOTTOM**

Just be sure to read the right entry for your choice!

3. Every now and then, you'll reach a part of the story that is decided by chance. This is called a "Challenge." Most of the time, you'll flip a coin to determine the outcome. Here's what a Challenge section looks like:

CHALLENGE!

Flip a coin and use the results to determine your path.

HEADS
If you land on heads, turn to **PAGE 17**

TAILS
If you land on tails, proceed to **PAGE 9**.

Depending on whether you get "heads" or "tails," simply turn to the indicated page and resume reading. In the example above, let's say you flip a coin and get "tails." In that case, turn to **PAGE 9** and continue the story.

That's all there is to it! Don't forget—when you finish one story, you can start over, make different choices, and create a whole new adventure! Now it's time to choose your first Pokémon—have fun!

EXPLORE THE GREAT OUTDOORS!

Welcome to Unova! There are so many natural wonders to explore here, from atop mountains to down by the seashore. No matter where you decide to travel, there are new Pokémon friends around every corner. As a Trainer and nature buff looking for adventure and wild Pokémon, you can find both in the remote outdoors. So, grab your canteen and put on your hiking boots because this journey takes you deep into the forests of Unova.

If you want to check out the ancient ruins in the valley, proceed to **page 27**.

To hike to Chargestone Cave, a spot many Electric-types call home, proceed to **page 10**.

If you'd like to take a scenic stroll and explore the woods, go to **page 22**.

TOP

You run down a corridor, hoping to find more Pokémon protectors of the ancient ruins. *Whish!* All of a sudden, you are hit with a gust of wind, or rather Cofagrigus' Ominous Wind. "Cofaaaaaaaaagriiiiiiiguuuuuuuus!" Cofagrigus warns you to stay away.

"Uh oh," you worry. This Cofagrigus thinks you're the bad guy.

To battle Cofagrigus right there, go to **page 38**.

To get Professor Jaan for backup, proceed to **page 51**.

BOTTOM

"We're just here to visit!" you plead. However, Cofagrigus can't hear you because it's in such a huff.

"Cof cof cof cof," Cofagrigus says, wrapping up you and Miller like mummies. Miller scans the floor looking for her Poké Ball. It's no use; even the floor is covered in wrappings. You have to get the Coffin Pokémon to calm down.

To see if Dewott can help you out of this mess, proceed to **page 13**.

To have Blitzle step in to stop Cofagrigus, go to **page 63**.

"Okay Dewott, we're going to walk slowly backward out of this cave together," you say, letting your Pokémon pal know your strategy.

Dewott nods its head, still hosing the rock with a steady stream of Water Gun. "Left, right, left right…" you instruct.

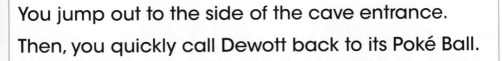

The rock rolls forward as you step backward, but Dewott's Water Gun keeps it at a safe distance. You're both about three feet from the cave's entrance. "Hold it here!" you tell Dewott.

You jump out to the side of the cave entrance. Then, you quickly call Dewott back to its Poké Ball.

The rock races forward and slams against the cave opening. It's too big to roll out of the entrance. Dewott's Water Gun saved the day!

You can't wait to have Dewott show off its strength in your next battle! So, you resume your journey, ready for more adventure…

THE END.

"Quick Shelmet, catch Miller in String Shot!" you plead.

"Shelllllmetttttt!" Shelmet shouts, shooting a slimy rope. However, Miller hears you and ducks out of the way. This time, you signal to Shelmet to try String Shot again! *Twhap!* Miller is stuck to the wall, thanks to Shelmet's good aim and gooey yarn.

Just then, Officer Jenny and Herdier arrive. "I see you two have already saved the day!" she says, thanking you. "Cof cof!" Cofagrigus cheers for you.

This isn't the first time Officer Jenny has had to chase after sticky-fingers Miller. Just last month, she snuck into the Nacrene City Museum. Although Officer Jenny protected the art, Miller slipped through her fingers. Now, thanks to you and Shelmet, Miller is caught! "We're happy to help!" you say.

"Shelllmet!" Shelmet agrees.

THE END.

You head up the mountain toward a camping ground. There you find a hungry Zweilous. Both heads are chowing down on all the food it has collected from campsites. It has a real sweet tooth! There are candy wrappers and soda cans everywhere. One of these soda cans must have slid down the mountain and into Klinklang's ring.

"It's good at gathering junk food—now Zweilous just needs to learn to take care of its trash," you decide. You tell Zweilous that you and your pals Gothorita and Dewott are here to help clean up the forest.

"Zweilous?" one head of Zweilous wonders. "Zweilous!" the other head of Zweilous insists.

With the power of teamwork, all of you clean up the woods in no time! "Way to go guys!" you say. "Zweilous!" it cheers.

You made such a good team that you decide to ask Zweilous if it wants to join you on your journey.

Proceed to **page 46**.

9

Chargestone Cave, Here We Come!

You just can't wait to see all the Electric-types charging up in Chargestone Cave's energy flow. As you step down the path, you can hear the low hum of electricity through the forest. You must be getting close to Chargestone Cave!

"Galvantulaaaaa!" Galvantula whispers. You turn your head and see a giant, fuzzy Galvantula crawling out of a bush. "Whoa, awesome!" you say in awe of the EleSpider Pokémon.

Of course, you want to try to catch the Bug- and Electric-type! You call on your pal Blitzle for backup.

To have Blitzle use Quick Attack, proceed to **page 19**.

To try Tail Whip, proceed to **page 32, top**.

You have to figure out a way to stop Litwick from starting another fire. So, you ask Dewott and Panpour to turn their Water Gun blasts on Litwick. "Liiiiiittttwiiiiiiiiick!" Litwick says, getting splashed. It's too tired to keep firing back.

"Swaaaaanna!" Swanna cheers, happy the battle and the blaze are over. You're happy you and Dewott could help! You say goodbye to your new Pokémon friends and head back toward the path.

"Pan pan!" Panpour says, running after you. Since you've shown what a good friend you are, Panpour wants to join you on your journey.

"We would love to have you come with us, buddy!" you say. "Deeeeewott!" Dewott agrees.

You toss your Poké Ball and catch your pal Panpour. You are so excited for more adventures together with your Pokémon friends!

You hear low hum of electric energy as you enter the cave. You take a good look around. The cave is crawling with incredible Electric-type Pokémon: Joltik, Galvantula, Tynamo, Klink, Klang, and more. You can't wait to show your Pokémon pals the scene!

"Galvantula, Blitzle, Stunfisk, you have to see this!" you say, tossing your Poké Balls.

"Stuuuuun…" Stunfisk says in awe.

Your Pokémon friends immediately feel energized by the electricity coming from the rocks. Heck, even you can almost feel the energy bursting from every corner!

"Gaaaaaalv!" Galvantula says, taking it all in.

Then, off in the distance you hear a clunking noise. Maybe it's just more Klink and Klang? Or maybe it's a cool machine, you wonder?

To leave the cave and continue on the journey, proceed to **page 62**.

To go investigate the noise, continue to **page 34**.

Just as you bring out Dewott, you have a stroke of genius. "Dewott, use your scalchops to cut these mummy wrappings to ribbons!" you instruct.

Dewott quickly leaps into action, displaying masterful skill in using its scalchops like blades. Almost instantly, Dewott reduces the mummy restraints to shreds. In the flurry of motion, the scraps of sliced cloth are swept into the air.

Miller gasps with relief as she is freed from her mummy coat. With the floor momentarily cleared of wrappings, she searches the floor for her Poké Ball. "Hooray, I found Karrablast!" she cheers. Realizing that you and Miller are no threat to the ancient ruins, Cofagrigus stops menacing you.

That's great news for Miller. It's even better news for you and your other Pokémon pal, Shelmet. "All we need is a trade machine and we can evolve our Pokémon together!" you explain.

Proceed to **page 45**.

13

You arrive at the Pokémon Center. There, Nurse Joy and her Audino greet you. You tell them about Blitzle's attempt to battle the wild Galvantula.

"Don't worry; Blitzle will be ready to battle again in no time!" Nurse Joy promises.

If you want to wait for Blitzle in the lobby, proceed to **page 26, top.**

To take a stroll and see if you can catch any wild Pokémon, go to **page 61.**

Using your Xtransciever, you call Professor Juniper. You explain Klinklang appears to be freaking out and its sparks have caused a forest fire. "What should I do?" you wonder.

Professor Juniper suggests you ask your Psychic-type pal Gothorita to use Charm. That should help Klinklang relax. "Great idea!" you say, taking out your Poké Ball. "Okay, Gothorita, let's see you use Charm!"

Gothorita gives it a try. Klinklang calms down and finally stops sparking. Now that it's still, you notice something is stuck in the Gear Pokémon.

"Don't worry, I'm here to help," you say, carefully approaching Klinklang. You discover an old soda can jammed in its ring. Now you want to find out who left this piece of trash lying around.

CHALLENGE!

Flip a coin and use the results to determine your path.

HEADS
If you land on heads, turn to **PAGE 17**.

TAILS
If you land on tails, proceed to **PAGE 9**.

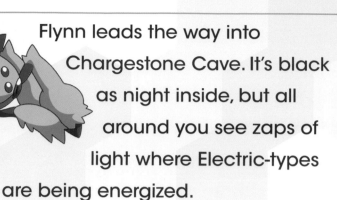

Flynn leads the way into Chargestone Cave. It's black as night inside, but all around you see zaps of light where Electric-types are being energized.

"This cave is so cool!" you tell Flynn. Then you toss your Poké Ball, adding, "You have to see this, Blitzle!"

"Blitzle!" your Pokémon companion says, instantly perking up in the free flowing electricity.

In no time, Blitzle is ready to battle again! You ask your new friends Flynn and Galvantula if they'd like a match. However, they came to Chargestone Cave to get ready for a battle at the local Pokémon Battle Club.

"Good luck! I hope our paths cross again someday," you say, wishing your new friend Flynn the best. "Then, the battle will be on!" Flynn says, shaking your hand.

"Galvantula!" Galvantula cheers.

THE END.

You follow a trail of trash down the mountain, hoping it will lead you to the culprit. "Who would treat nature like it's a trash can?" you wonder. You hear a rustle, so you run toward the sound.

"Gaarrrrrrrrr!" Garbodor, the Trash Heap Pokémon, cries.

Even for Garbodor, it's trailing a lot of trash. A bunch of its garbage is tangled up in some bushes. It can hardly move, the poor thing! It must have passed through a dump or got caught in a trash pile. Whatever happened, it needs your help, and you're always happy to pitch in. You help to free it from the bushes.

"Gar gar," Garbodor thanks you.

"How about I take you to Nurse Joy to get cleaned up?" you offer.

Proceed to **page 28**.

"I have an idea," you say excitedly. "Keep up the good work, Stunfisk!" You have your pals Gothorita and Dewott join Stunfisk. Teamwork gets the job done, and it's so much more fun!

"Dewott, fill the bowls with Water Gun!" you ask. "Dewooooooooottttttt!" Dewott says, making a splash.

Then you ask Gothorita to use its Psychic-type moves to levitate the bowls and pour out the water over the flames. "Goooooooothooooooooriiiiiiiiiiitaaaaaaaaaaa!" it sings as it follows your instructions.

Soon, the blaze is completely out. Litwick is so shocked, it holds its fire. "Way to go team!" you cheer. Now you have one thing on your mind: catching another Pokémon friend!

To try to catch the wild Swanna, proceed to **page 49, top**.

To try to catch the wild Litwick, turn to **page 33**.

Blitzle bursts into battle mode with Quick Attack. Galvantula is unable to dodge it. Blitzle then warms up for Flame Charge. "Bliitzle!" Blitzle yelps, running with a trail of fire.

While Galvantula tries to dodge Blitzle, you think fast and toss your Poké Ball. "Sweet!" you cheer, catching the Electric- and Bug-type Pokémon.

You realize Galvantula and Blitzle must be tired from the battle. So, you decide to let them recharge by basking in Chargestone Cave.

As you hike down the path, you hear "Jol jol jol…" A pack of Joltik say this as they scurry past you. You must be getting close! Through the brush, you see Chargestone Cave, but it has two entrances. Which way should you go?

Flip a coin and use the results to determine your path.

 HEADS If you land on heads, turn to **PAGE 37**.

 TAILS If you land on tails, proceed to **PAGE 12**.

Blitzle and Tynamo are both fast, but Tynamo surprises you with a speedy start.

"Tynamooooooooo!" Tynamo says, shooting a yellow Thunderbolt streak straight at Blitzle. Thanks to its Motor Drive Ability, your pal speeds up when the Electric-type move hits it. So, you suggest Quick Attack because it's a Normal-type move.

"Blitzleeeeeeee!" Blitzle launches the attack. However, Tynamo dodges it and now Blitzle is tired.

"Now, use Charge Beam!" Professor Jaan suggests. With that strong move, Tynamo wins the round. Like a good sport, you congratulate your new friends on their win.

"It was a pleasure to battle a Trainer brave enough to catch a thief! Someday you'll be one of the best because of your courage," Professor Jaan adds. You head back out on your journey, ready to work hard and prove the Professor right!

THE END.

Dylan starts the battle by instructing Mandibuzz to swoop in with Aerial Ace. "Mandibuzzzzzz!" Mandibuzz says, shooting down from the sky.

However, Stunfisk flips out of the way at the last second. "All right!" you cheer. "Now, use Thundershock."

"Stunfisssssskkk!" your Pokémon yelps, unleashing a zap of electricity.

Mandibuzz gets caught in the shock and tries to fly away. Before it can make its next move, you tell Stunfisk to shoot a Thunderbolt up into the sky. *Whap!* With that powerful jolt of electricity, you and Stunfisk have won the round. Hooray!

"Thank you for such a great battle," you say, shaking Dylan's hand.

"Sure was better than sitting in the lobby!" Dylan jokes. With that, you two return to the Pokémon Center to pick up your friends.

THE END.

Where There's Smoke, There's Fire

The sun rises over your camp atop a mountain. From this height, you can see Unova's lush forests for miles. You take a deep breath to smell the fresh, crisp air on this sunny morning. It's the perfect day for a hike.

You pack up your supplies and start down the mountain. It's rocky at first, but soon the path leads you into some tall trees.

You notice a bunch of Emolga are gliding from treetop to treetop. Then, a group of forest Pokémon—Deerling, Watchog, Lilligant, and Cottonee—all fly past you heading up the mountain. They're in quite a hurry.

"Hmm, something weird is going on here," you think. Suddenly, you smell a waft of smoke. "Oh no, there must be a fire!" you reason.

To head down the mountain to try to find the source of the blaze, proceed to **page 32, bottom**.

To go to the lake to figure out a way to hose off the area, go to **page 42**.

You spot Miller running toward you. "So glad you're here!" you say, relieved.

However, she runs straight past you into the cave. Oh no! She's headed straight for some golden treasure. It looks like you accidentally helped a thief.

"She's not going to get away with this! Not on my watch," you promise. You think fast to come up with a plan.

To have Shelmet trap the trickster with String Shot, go to **page 8**.

If you think the best bet is to have Cofagrigus handle the problem, go to **page 35**.

23

"Tynamooooooo!" Tynamo yelps, starting the battle with Charge Beam. Dewott jumps out of the attack's path at the last second. "Nice one!" you cheer.

You tell Dewott to gather its energy with Focus Energy and then attack with its scalchops using Razor Shell. "Dew dewott!" Dewott says, taking aim. Swoosh! Razor Shell slashes the air as it hits Tynamo to win the battle.

"You two are amazing!" Professor Jaan says, congratulating you and Dewott on the match. You thank Professor Jaan for the round. You can't wait to get back on the road and see the next adventure Unova has in store for you!

THE END.

"Gothorita, help!"
you shout, tossing your
Poké Ball. First, Gothorita
uses Charm to help
Crustle chill out.

"Crussssstle," Crustle
sighs, starting to relax under Gothorita's spell.

Then Gothorita bathes you in a purple light.
You feel yourself lifting up, off Crustle, and
Gothorita's glow slowly carries you back down
to the ground. While Crustle is still hypnotized by
Gothorita, you think fast and toss a Poké Ball.

"Awesome!" you cheer as you catch Crustle.
"Gothorita, you're amazing. I couldn't have done
it without you!"

"Goth goth," Gothorita says, blushing from your praise.

You head back to the Pokémon Center with your
new friend Crustle. You can't wait to introduce it to
your friend Blitzle!

THE END.

"Hi, I'm Dylan," says a boy waiting in the lobby, introducing himself. While you're both waiting, you decide to have a battle! You step outside into a field next to the Pokémon Center.

"I choose you, Mandibuzz!" Dylan says, throwing his Poké Ball.

You take out your Pokédex. It tells you Mandibuzz, the Bone Vulture Pokémon, is a Dark- and Flying-type. Which one of your Pokémon pals do you want to choose?

To battle with Stunfisk, go to **page 21**.

To choose Gothorita, go to **page 41**.

"Stunfisk!" Stunfisk cheers, ready to help. Use Mud Slap to stop Litwick!" you instruct.

Stunfisk fires a big, brown dirt blob. As the mud hits Litwick's flame, it cooks like clay against Litwick's round body and turns into bowls. "Whoa!" you say with surprise.

Continue to **page 18**.

"Brav-braviary!" Braviary says, taking flight with Dewott. With teamwork, the two Pokémon extinguish the blaze in no time. "Way to go!" Reeden cheers.

Now Dewott and Braviary turn their attention to Litwick. They want to make sure it won't accidentally cause another fire. Dewott shoots another burst of Water Gun. "Litwiiiiick!" it says, dodging the stream.

"Braviary, add Whirlwind!" Reeden says, thinking on her feet. Braviary's Whirlwind gust sprays the water everywhere, and Litwick can't run from it. Thanks to some clever teamwork, Litwick's fiery flame is no longer a danger.

"Swanna swan!" Swanna thanks you all for the help.

To battle to catch Swanna, proceed to **page 55**.

If you want to ask your new friend Reeden for a battle, go to **page 44, top**.

31

"Bliiiiiitz!" Blitzle shrieks as it tries a distracting waggle of Tail Whip to lower Galvantula's defenses. Galvantula uses its front feelers to grab Blitzle.

"Try to slip out!" you shout. It's no use. Blitzle is drained of its energy. The supercharged Galvantula scurries off into the woods leaving you with one tired Blitzle.

To head to the Pokémon Center so Blitzle can get some rest, turn to **page 14**.

To continue exploring Chargestone Cave, proceed to **page 30**.

You race down the mountainside, following the smoke all the way into the valley. The air is thick, so you pull up your shirt collar as a mask to cover your nose. You're so close, but you can't get any closer. So you take out your binoculars to see if you can spot the problem.

You see a Klinklang shooting off flaming sparks from its silver spikes. That must be what's causing this fire. How can you stop Klinklang?!

To call Professor Juniper for advice, go to **page 15**.

To battle Klinklang, go to **page 36**.

"Litwiiiiiiiick!" Litwick sighs, too tired to keep battling. It expended all of its energy firing moves. You think fast and toss your Poké Ball.

However, it doesn't work! All of a sudden, you hear… "Litwick, there you are!" says a tall girl named Lucky. "I've been so worried."

"Liiiiiiiiiitwick," Litwick exclaims, hugging its Trainer.

When Lucky woke up this morning, Litwick was missing. Litwick and Lucky lost their last couple battles, and they have a big Gym battle tomorrow. Litwick was just trying to get as strong as possible so it wouldn't disappoint its Trainer again.

"All you have to do is try your best tomorrow! I love you no matter what happens," Lucky promises. Litwick is so relieved. The pair are off to Nurse Joy so Litwick can rest up for the Gym battle tomorrow.

"Good luck!" you wish your new friends. Then you hit the dusty trail to continue your journey.

THE END.

You follow the noise deep into the cave until you reach a circular room. The sound is strong so you swirl your flashlight around the room, but you don't see any entrances. Blitzle has an idea.

Blitzle uses Flame Charge to race around the room. Thanks to Blitzle's light trail, you spot a small crawl space. The sound seems like it's coming from there! "Tynamoooo!" the Elefish Pokémon says, flying out of the hole.

"Hi, I'm Poppy," a girl with short purple hair says, crawling out after Tynamo. She has a contraption in her hand that is blinking and buzzing. That's where the sound was coming from! She made an Electro-Reader machine to measure the amount of power in the cave. Now her machine is on the fritz. "Maybe I should take a break," she says. "Would you like to battle me and Tynamo?" Which Pokémon pal do you want to choose?

To use Galvantula, go to **page 39**.

Go to **page 54** to use Blitzle.

"Coffffaaaaa!"
Cofagrigus says,
staring you down.
You try to point
Cofagrigus in Miller's
direction, but it just won't
listen to you. Just then,
a man wearing a vest and tie comes running up.

"Hi, I'm Professor Jaan," he says, introducing himself. He studies the ruins, and his computer has detected some weird heat readings. You explain that Miller is up to no good and Cofagrigus has you trapped.

"So glad you're here to help!" you confess.

Professor Jaan instructs Cofagrigus to leave you alone. You're amazed at how the Coffin Pokémon listens to its friend Professor Jaan. Now it's time to go after the real culprit: Miller.

To team to up with Professor Jaan and Cofagrigus to catch Miller, continue to **page 56**.

To try to find some more Cofagrigus or Sigilyph for backup, proceed to **page 6, top**.

"Dewott, I choose you!" you say, tossing your Poké Ball. "Deeeeeeewott!" Dewott says, ready to help.

To hose down this situation, you ask Dewott to use Water Gun. The blast turns the fire into steam with a sizzle. "Awesome! Add Aqua Jet," you advise.

Dewott's next attack hits its mark, and Klinklang is unable to battle. Just then, Officer Jenny pulls up on her motorcycle to investigate the fire. "Don't worry," you say, "Dewott has saved the day!"

"Nice work," Officer Jenny says, thanking you and your Pokémon pal. Then, you take your Dewott for a well-deserved rest at the Pokémon Center.

THE END.

You pick the entrance that you think leads into Chargestone Cave. Big, pointy rocks called stalactites cover the ceiling. They look kind of like teeth, so the cave looks almost like a mouth carved out of a mountain.

You touch the rock wall to see if you can sense the energy flow. However, you don't feel a thing. You decide to walk further into the cave, but it's deep and dark. You open the screen on your Pokédex to use its light to find your way. However, before you can take another step, you hear a giant crash in the distance. The ground starts shaking. Could it be an earthquake?

All of a sudden, you see a giant stalactite rock rolling toward you. "Uh-oh!" you worry. You have to think fast and stop it!

To have Dewott use Water Gun to stop the rock with its blast, go to **page 57, top**.

To have Shelmet use its sticky spit to stop the rock in its tracks, go to **page 48**.

"I choose you, Stunfisk!" you say, calling on your pal for help. "Quick, use Mud Bomb."

"Stuuuuuunfisk!" Stunfisk shouts, aiming a big, brown blob at the Coffin Pokémon. "Cofaaaaaa." Cofagrigus moans in confusion because it can't see through all the mud.

While it's weak, you think fast and toss your Poké Ball. Not only have you stopped the attack, you've also caught a new friend. "All right!" you cheer. "Now, it's time to go back and help Professor Jaan!"

Continue to **page 58**.

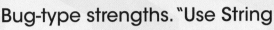

All of you head to a patch of grass outside the cave. Galvantula is ready to go! You start by playing to its Bug-type strengths. "Use String Shot!" you suggest. "Gaaaaaaaal!" Galvantula says, wrapping Tynamo in its sticky string.

Before Tynamo can break loose, you have Galvantula get its claws around the slippery Pokémon to drain its energy. "Tyyyyyynammooooo," it sighs, getting tired. Galvantula wins the battle!

"You two electrify the battlefield!" Poppy says, congratulating you and Galvantula. You wish her the best of luck with her research at Chargestone Cave. "I'm looking forward to learning more about this special place," Poppy says.

"Well, I've found that it's also great for making new friends," you say. Then you head back down the path to see what other adventures Unova has in store for you!

THE END.

"Deeeeeeeeewooooooooottttttt!"
Dewott cries, spraying a huge
stream of Water Gun. Just then,
a Trainer wearing glasses
comes running up. "Hi, I'm
Reeden," she says. "I'm here
to help!"

Boy, does she have a brilliant idea! She offers to
have her pal Braviary fly Dewott around while it
hoses off the forest. This way, it can travel far
and fast!

"That's a great idea!" you say.
"Sound good, Dewott?"

"Dewott!" Dewott says, nodding
its head.

"All right, Braviary, we're counting on
you!" Reeden says, tossing her Poké Ball.

Proceed to **page 31**.

You decide to make the first move. You bet Gothorita can throw off Mandibuzz with Confusion, but it flies out of range. "Mandibuuuuuuuzzzzzzzz!" Mandibuzz cries, swooping in to surprise Gothorita with Aerial Ace.

"Goth!" Gothorita yelps as it's knocked off balance. "Gothorita, use Psybeam!" you instruct.

However, Mandibuzz confuses Gothorita with Double Team. Gothorita doesn't know where to shoot its attack. "Maaaaaaaaandibuzz!" Mandibuzz shouts, releasing a strong Air Slash that wins the round.

"Wow, you and Mandibuzz are an incredible team!" you tell Dylan.

Dylan thanks you for the battle. Then, you and your new pal head back to the Pokémon Center. You can't wait to get back on the road because you know more fun battles are in store!

THE END.

Down at the lake, you see a whole flock of sleepy Swanna napping at the shore. However, one brave Swanna is battling a fierce Litwick with a giant flame. "What is going on?" you wonder.

It looks like Litwick sapped the energy from the flock of Swanna. Now Litwick is super strong, and one daring Swanna is fighting back for its flock.

Swanna is doing its best in battle, but as the extra powerful Litwick attacks, its massive Fire-type moves are setting the woods ablaze. Good thing you're here in time to help Swanna!

To act fast and choose Stunfisk to step in and battle Litwick, proceed to **page 26, bottom**.

To have Dewott hose down the fire, proceed to **page 57, bottom**.

Bisharp begins by trying to use Fury Cutter.
However, Stunfisk dodges at the last second.
You shout, "Stunfisk, move in with Mud-Slap."

"Stuuuuuunfisk!" it yelps,
kicking mud toward Bisharp.
Bisharp is covered in the goop.
You have Stunfisk follow up with
Mud Bomb. "Bishaaaaaarp,"
Bisharp huffs, unable
to continue.

"Congratulations," Miller
says, shaking your hand
like a good sport. "I hope
our paths cross again in Unova,"
you say. "When they do,
I'll be ready for a rematch!"
Miller promises.

You smile and wave goodbye to your new pal.
Energized by the battle, you and Stunfisk are ready
for more fun and friends!

You ask Reeden if she's up for a battle. However, the sun is about to set and she wants to set up her camp.

"I would love to battle you some other time!" Reeden promises.

You decide to head to the campsite with your new pal. You can roast marshmallows, trade stories, and really get to know your new friend. It's so nice to make a new buddy that you know you can count on!

THE END.

"You know, I've never seen Tynamo before," you admit to Professor Jaan.

"Well, I'll do you one better. Let's have a battle," he offers.

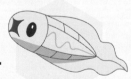

"Awesome!" you cheer.

To choose Dewott, proceed to **page 24**.

To choose Blitzle, go to **page 20**.

44

You and Miller travel to the Pokémon Center to borrow a special trade machine from Nurse Joy.

"This is going to work perfectly!" you say, barely able to contain your excitement. As the machine is activated, there's a burst of light. When it clears, two evolved Pokémon—Accelgor and Escavalier—stand before you and Miller. "Yay, it worked!" you cheer.

You, Accelgor and your new friends Miller and Escavalier head to a clearing in the woods. "All right, here, we go!" Miller signals.

Escavalier starts the match with Twineedle. Accelgor responds with Leech Life, but Escavalier dodges it. So Accelgor lunges forward with a Quick Attack to win the round!

Miller thanks you for all your help. "That's what friends are for," you add. You wish Miller and Escavalier well as you continue your journey. You just can't wait for your next battle with Accelgor!

You're so excited to get to battle Zweilous, the Hostile Pokémon. Certainly, it should put up a good fight. "Zweilooooooous!" it cries, starting the battle with Dragon Rush.

Dewott is able to dodge the explosion. "Way to go! Now use Water Gun," you shout. "Deeeeeeewoooooooottttt!" Dewott yelps, unleashing quite a blast.

While Zweilous is dripping with water and can't quite see through its bangs, you have Dewott add Razor Shell. Zweilous doesn't even see those scalchops flying toward it, so you decide it's time to toss your Poké Ball!

"Hooray!" you cheer, thrilled to have caught the Dark- and Dragon-type Pokémon. Now it's time to take out the trash and give your new friends a rest at the Pokémon Center.

You call on Dewott to help you battle Crustle. "Use Water Gun!" you instruct. "Dewoooooooott!" Dewott shouts, shooting a stream of water.

However, the blast lands right between Crustle's eyes. It can't see anything, so now it's just trying to shake you off. You do your best to keep your balance, but when Crustle stops short, you go flying.

"Whooooooooaaaa!" you yelp. Luckily, you land in some tall bushes. Dewott helps you climb down.

"Thanks for all your help, buddy," you say.

"Deeeewott," Dewott says, glad that you're A-okay.

Too bad that cool Crustle scurried off; you would have liked to try to catch it. Oh well, you're glad to have friends like Dewott and Blitzle. Speaking of Blitzle, you can't wait to pick up your pal from the Pokémon Center. Blitzle will be so happy to see you!

THE END.

"Shellllllmet!" Shelmet says, as you send it out. It unleashes a wave of its goopy saliva. *Whap!* It slaps the side of the stalactite. The rock can't roll forward because it is caught in the glue-like Shelmet spit. "Phew!" you let out a sigh of relief. "That sure was a close one."

You and Shelmet hightail it out of there. Then, once you're safely back in the woods, you thank Shelmet for helping you. "Shelmet shel!" Shelmet says, happy it could save the day.

You decide not to risk trying the other cave entrance with no guarantee that it's the real Chargestone Cave. Instead, you decide to take Galvantula to the Pokémon Center where it's guaranteed to get a good rest, without any more rocky drama.

THE END.

You ask the amazing Swanna if it would like to battle. "Swanna!" Swanna says excitedly.

To choose Shelmet for the battle, go to **page 52**.

To use Blitzle, go to **page 29**.

Swanna joins its pack for their daily ritual, a dance at dusk. They wave their elegant wings and shake their tail feathers. The White Bird Pokémon perform a beautiful routine around the lake. "Bravo!" you cheer, clapping for the incredible performance.

Then you say goodbye to your new friend Swanna. You head back out on your journey, excited to spot more wild Pokémon!

THE END.

You call on Blitzle to give Dewott a ride out of the cave while it shoots Water Gun. "Bli blitzle!" Blitzle says, ready for the challenge.

Dewott hops on Blitzle and maintains a steady Water Gun stream to make sure the rock doesn't get any closer. Together, all of you are able to exit the cave.

"Dewwwwwooooottt!" Dewott says, keeping up the Water Gun hose. It's afraid to stop, because the rock will keep rolling. You have to stop the rock for good, but how?!

You think fast and instruct, "Quick, Blitzle, use Stomp to make a ditch inside the cave."

Blitzle snaps into action and digs its hooves into the ground. Then, as it runs out of the cave, the rock rolls forward. *Boom!* The rock is stuck in the ditch.

"Way to go team!" you cheer. That sure was a close one.

"Professor, help!" you shout as Cofagrigus chases you. Cofagrigus listens to Professor Jaan and immediately focuses on the real thief. Relieved, you call on your pal Gothorita to help Tynamo and Cofagrigus.

However, suddenly Miller cries, "I'm so sorry." She explains she just wanted to snatch an ancient artifact she heard about, a Cosmic Strength Stone. Miller tells you she has never won a battle or caught a Pokémon. She hoped the artifact would make her Tepig stronger so they could finally taste success.

"However, the Cosmic Strength Stone is just a myth," Professor Jaan explains. "You can't steal your way to victory; it takes hard work and practice!"

You offer to take Miller to the nearest Pokémon Battle Club. "Don George will help you train to be a champion," you promise. Happy for some help, Miller heads out of the cave with you. Professor Jaan adds, "Good luck to you both!"

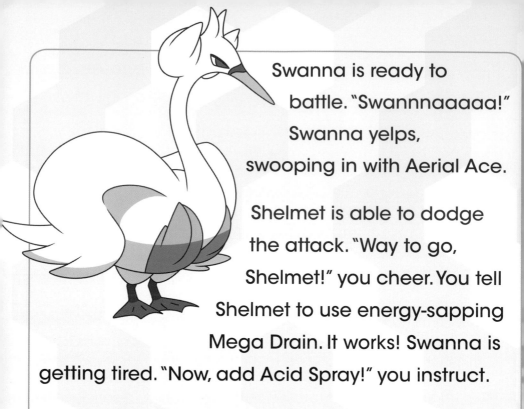

Swanna is ready to battle. "Swannnaaaaa!" Swanna yelps, swooping in with Aerial Ace.

Shelmet is able to dodge the attack. "Way to go, Shelmet!" you cheer. You tell Shelmet to use energy-sapping Mega Drain. It works! Swanna is getting tired. "Now, add Acid Spray!" you instruct.

"Shelllllmeeeeeeet!" Shelmet cries out, shooting a green spray. With that, Swanna is unable to battle. You think fast and toss your Poké Ball.

"Hooray!" you cheer, excited to catch your new Water- and Flying-type friend. You thank your pal Shelmet for its awesome battle moves. Then you head back on your journey, even more prepared for adventure.

THE END.

"Deeeeeew!" Dewott yelps, kicking off the battle with an Aqua Jet attack. Although Dewott slams straight into Bisharp, the opponent quickly shrugs it off.

"Bisharp, use Metal Claw," Miller responds. "Bisssssssharp-harp-harp," Bisharp says, swiping at Dewott.

"Try soaking Bisharp in Water Gun," you suggest to Dewott.

Dewott hits Bisharp with a blast of water, but Miller has a clever idea. "Now, use Metal Burst!" Miller instructs. With Bisharp's own power multiplied and thrown straight back at it, Dewott is too weak to keep battling.

Like a good sport, you shake your new friend Miller's hand and thank her for the awesome match. Even if you didn't win the round, you're happy to have won a new friend.

THE END.

You and Poppy head to a clearing in the woods. "Tynamo, use Spark!" Poppy says, starting the battle. Quick on its feet, Blitzle dodges it. Then you ask it to add Flame Charge. However, slippery Tynamo speeds away. "Try Discharge," you suggest. *Zap!* Tynamo is caught in a blast of electricity.

"Tynamo, we can use Discharge too," Poppy shouts. *Whap!* Now Blitzle is caught in an electrical flare. Then, both you and Poppy tell your Pokémon pals to use Thunderbolt.

Wham! The double Thunderbolt sends a huge blast of light into the sky. There is so much energy in the explosion that both Blitzle and Tynamo are too wiped out to keep battling. Strangely enough, Poppy's Electro Reader stops beeping. The Thunderbolt blast fully recharged its batteries.

"Guess it just needed some juice," Poppy laughs. She thanks you and Blitzle for a fun battle. More adventure awaits you and your Pokémon!

You ask Swanna to battle. "Swanna!" it cheers, ready for some fun.

"Shelmet, I choose you!" you say, tossing your Poké Ball. You ask Shelmet to kick off the battle with Leech Life. Swanna doesn't even flinch.

"Try Acid," you suggest to Shelmet. "Sheeeelmet!" Shelmet cries, unleashing the purple stream. However, Swanna still stays strong.

Then, the White Bird Pokémon uses a bursting blue BubbleBeam. "Swanaaaaaaaaaaa!" Swanna yelps, adding a fierce Air Slash attack.

Shelmet is too tired to keep battling after Swanna's strong attacks. However, Swanna is still full of energy! Furthermore, the sun is setting, which is a very important time for Swanna.

Proceed to **page 49, bottom**.

You, Professor Jaan and Cofagrigus catch up to Miller in a painted room deep in the ancient ruins. She has stolen a gold statue of Sigilyph.

Professor Jaan calls on his pal Tynamo. You choose Stunfisk. Together with Cofagrigus, you're ready to catch a thief! So, Miller takes out her Woobat to battle. "Wooooooo!" Woobat cries when it sees the competition.

Then, Woobat flies out of the ancient ruins, scared stiff. "Get back here!" Miller says, chasing Woobat. However, Officer Jenny is waiting for Miller at the exit. Officer Jenny nabs the thief red-handed.

"You guys are true heroes for helping me catch sticky-fingers Miller," Officer Jenny says to you and Professor Jaan. "Aw shucks, I just wanted to do the right thing!" you say.

Proceed to **page 44, bottom**.

You send out Dewott. It shouts "Dewoooooooooott!" as it unleashes a Water Gun blast. The shot of water is so powerful, the rock slows down. However, how can you make your escape if Dewott has to keep spraying Water Gun? You aren't even sure how long Dewott can keep blasting. You have to think fast!

If you want to try to slowly step out of the cave and then return Dewott to its Poké Ball, go to **page 7**.

If you want to have Dewott keep firing Water Gun as it rides out on Blitzle, go to **page 50**.

BOTTOM

"Deeeeeewwwww—" Dewott says, preparing to shoot Water Gun at the blaze.

"Wait!" you say, stopping Dewott just before it can make its watery move. You hear a rustling in the bushes. What could it be?

To investigate, proceed to **page 59**.

To have Dewott go ahead and use Water Gun, turn to **page 40**.

Professor Jaan and Tynamo are fighting the good fight! They're caught in an intense battle with Miller and Drilbur. While Miller focuses on the clash, you decide to sneak up on her with Shelmet.

"Tie her up in String Shot," you whisper. Shelmet aims a gluey String Shot lasso and catches Miller.
"Good work!" Professor Jaan thanks you and Shelmet.

"I got your alert, Professor," Officer Jenny says, running up. "However, I see you two have already handled the trouble." Officer Jenny thanks you all for your courage as she escorts the thief out of the cave.

Then, Professor Jaan takes you on a special tour of the ruin's ancient wall paintings.

"Amazing!" you say, taking it all in. Unova has such a rich history! You can't wait to make your own mark here. You thank the Professor and set back out on your journey.

THE END.

You tiptoe up to the bushes. You pull back a branch and peak over the brush.

"Pa-pa-pa-pa-panpooooouuuuuur!" a sad Panpour whimpers. It's scared of fire and all alone. "Aw, don't worry Panpour," you say. "I'm here to help!"

Panpour is happy you've come to rescue it. However, that's when you have a great idea. You bet Water-type Panpour can rescue itself *and* the forest!

"Panpour and Dewott, use Water Gun to put out the blaze," you suggest. Together, they hose off the forest and save the day.

"Great teamwork!" you congratulate them.
"Panpour!" the once shy Panpour says, proud of itself.

Continue to **page 11**.

You muster up all your courage and walk into the ancient ruins. It's so quiet you could hear a pin drop. You feel a presence behind you.

"Aaaaah!" you scream, realizing Cofagrigus has snuck up on you. "Cofagriiiiiiigus!" Cofagrigus shrieks. You call in backup: Blitzle. "Use Shock Wave fast!" you ask.

Cofagrigus soars away from Blitzle's attack. Then it swoops back in to deliver a stunning Mean Look. Blitzle is caught in its gaze, so Cofagrigus adds Shadow Ball.

"Bliiiiiiiii," Blitzle sighs, unable to keep battling clever Cofagrigus. Before you can take out another Poké Ball, Cofagrigus has you wrapped up like a mummy.

Proceed to **page 23**.

You decide to head out into the woods to see if you can spot any wild Pokémon. You see little rock ledge in some bushes. You figure you can get a better vantage point to spot Pokémon if you're a few more feet up in the air. However, as you hop atop the rock, it starts to move.

"Wha-wha-whoa!" you say, trying not to tumble off the rock. You discover that it's not a rock after all—it's a Crustle!

"Crus crus crus," Crustle says, looking frustrated. You startled Crustle, and now it really wants you off its back. In fact, it's starting to move and shake. It might even use a move!

"How am I going to get down now?!" you wonder.

If you want to call on Gothorita to help you levitate to the ground, proceed to **page 25**.

To try to battle Crustle to get it to need to rest, proceed to **page 47**.

With all of your Electric-type Pokémon fully charged thanks to Chargestone Cave, you're ready for more adventure! Where would you like to go next?

You know there are some incredible ancient ruins close by.

To visit the ancient ruins, proceed to **page 27**.

To see what wild Pokémon come your way on a hike through the woods, go to **page 22**.

"Blitzle, try Flame Charge!" you suggest. Blitzle runs around the room leaving a trail of yellow light. The bright flame gets Cofagrigus' attention. It shines on the ground so you and Miller can get a better look.

Miller scurries to snag a round lump in the corner. She dusts it off. "All right!" she cheers, holding her Poké Ball. Cofagrigus, seeing that you and Miller meant no harm, stops trying to wrap you up. "Now that I have Bisharp back, how about a battle?"

"I'm always up for a match!" you say, ready to go.

To choose Dewott go to **page 53**.

To choose Stunfisk, proceed to **page 43**.

Glossary

acknowledge
respond; answer; admit

artifact
relic; an object that has
historical or cultural interest

backup
help; support; assistance

basking
lounging; relaxing

buff
admirer; fan; expert

culprit
guilty person; criminal;
wrongdoer

disappoint
to let somebody down;
sadden

distracting
taking somebody's attention
away from what he or she is
doing; confusing

escort
to accompany, lead,
or shepherd

exclaim
shout; cry out; yell

expend
use up; spend; pay out

extinguish
smother; put out; quench

flare
a sudden blaze of light or
fire; flash; sparkle

flurry
burst of activity; gust

frustrated
upset; annoyed; bothered

furthermore
also; additionally

hightail
to leave quickly; rush away
from a place

intense
strong; powerful; extreme

maintain
to make something
continue; to preserve

massive
huge; gigantic; enormous

masterful
showing expert skill or
ability

menacing
bullying; scaring;
threatening

multiplied
increased by a large amount;
enlarged; magnified

on the fritz
not working properly; out of
order; broken

pitch in
to help or cooperate

red-handed
in the act of doing
something wrong

remote
far away; distant; isolated

restraints
something that prevents or
limits movement; chains;
bonds; belts

resume
start again; continue

routine
a rehearsed or practiced
performance

saliva
spit; drool; slobber

stalactite
a column, spike,
or pillar hanging from
the roof or ceiling

tiptoe
to move cautiously or
quietly; sneak

unleash
to release; set free

vantage point
a position that provides a
broad view of something;
point of view

Index

Accelgor 45

ancient ruins 5, 6, 27, 35, 56, 60, 62

Audino 14

Bisharp 43, 53, 63

Blitzle 10, 12, 14, 16, 19, 20, 25, 27, 29, 30, 32, 34, 44, 47, 49, 50, 54, 57, 60, 63

Braviary 31, 40

Chargestone Cave 5, 10, 16, 19, 30, 32, 37, 39, 48, 62

Cofagrigus 6, 8, 23, 27, 35, 38, 51, 56, 60, 63

Cottonee 22

Crustle 25, 47, 61

Deerling 22

Dewott 7, 9, 11, 13, 18, 24, 31, 33, 36, 37, 40, 42, 44, 46, 47, 50, 53, 57, 59, 63

Don George 51

Drilbur 58

Dylan 21, 26, 41

Emolga 22

Escavalier 45

Flynn 16, 30

Galvantula 10, 12, 14, 16, 19, 30, 32, 34, 39, 48

Garbodor 17, 28

Gothorita 9, 15, 18, 25, 26, 33, 41, 51, 61

Herdier 8

Joltik 12, 19

Karrablast 13

Klang 12

Klink 12

Klinklang 9, 15, 32, 36

Lilligant 22

Litwick 11, 18, 26, 31, 33, 42

Lucky 33

Mandibuzz 21, 26, 41

Miller 6, 8, 13, 23, 27, 35, 43, 45, 51, 53, 56, 58, 63

Nacrene City Museum 8

Nurse Joy 14, 17, 28, 33, 45, 47

Officer Jenny 8, 36, 56, 58

Panpour 11, 59

Poké Ball 7, 11, 12, 13, 15, 16, 19, 25, 26, 27, 28, 29, 33, 36, 38, 40, 46, 52, 55, 57, 60, 63

Pokédex 26, 37

Pokémon Battle Club 16, 51

Pokémon Center 14, 21, 25, 26, 28, 32, 36, 41, 45, 46, 47, 48

Poppy 34, 39, 54

Professor Jaan 6, 20, 24, 35, 38, 44, 51, 56, 58

Reeden 31, 40, 44

Shelmet 8, 13, 23, 37, 48, 49, 52, 55, 58

Sigilyph 27, 35, 56

Stunfisk 12, 18, 21, 26, 28, 38, 42, 43, 56, 63

Swanna 11, 18, 29, 31, 42, 49, 52, 55

Tepig 51

Tynamo 12, 20, 24, 34, 39, 44, 51, 54, 56, 58

Unova 5, 22, 24, 27, 39, 43, 58

Watchog 22

Woobat 56

Xtransciever 15

Zweilous 9, 46

Attack at the Ancient Ruins

Unova's ancient ruins are legendary, and you hope you're about to see them up close. Some say that these ruins hold treasure! Just as you approach the cave entrance, Miller, a woman with curly hair, comes running out.

"Aaaaaaaaaaaack!" Miller screams as if she just saw a ghost.

She tells you that she too came to explore the ancient ruins, but got chased out by Cofagrigus. It was using its Shadow Ball attack, so she had to make a break for it.

"Wait, where's my Poké Ball?" she says, digging through her pockets. "Oh no, it must have fallen out when I was running!" Always there for someone in need, you bravely offer to help Miller.

To use your Blitzle to run around and distract Cofagrigus, proceed to **page 60**.

To try to reason with Cofagrigus so it will let Miller look for the lost Poké Ball, go to **page 6, bottom**.

At the Pokémon Center, Nurse Joy helps Garbodor get cleaned up. You thank her for her help. However, now you have one thing on your mind: catching your new Pokémon pal! So you ask it for a battle. "Garrrrrbodor!" Garbodor says excitedly.

You head to a field and take out your Poké Ball. "I choose you, Stunfisk!" you shout.

Garbodor starts with Sludge Bomb, but Stunfisk flops out of its way. "Way to go, Stunfisk! Now, stun Garbodor with ThunderShock," you instruct.

Garbodor stops in place. While it's stunned, you tell Stunfisk to add a Mud Bomb attack. Then you toss your Poké Ball. "Yay!" you cheer, happy you caught your new friend. "Thanks for all your help Stunfisk."

"Stuuuuuunfisk," Stunfisk says with a proud smile. Then you continue your journey. You can't wait for your next battle!

THE END.

"Are you up for a battle?" you ask your new friend Swanna. "Swaaaaanna!" Swanna says, ready to play.

"I choose you, Blitzle!" you say, tossing your Poké Ball.

Swanna starts the battle by swooping in with Aerial Ace, but speedy Blitzle outruns the attack.

"Bliiiiiitzleeeee!" Blitzle says, shooting a Thunder Wave zap. "Add Shock Wave!" you suggest.

With that powerful combination, you win the battle! However, now you want to see if you can catch your new friend Swanna. You toss your Poké Ball.

"Yay!" you cheer, excited that Swanna will join you on your journey. Then you thank your buddy Blitzle for the awesome battle. You can't wait to start training with your new Pokémon pal.

THE END.

From a cliff, you spot the famous Chargestone Cave. "Look at that!" you say excitedly as you watch Electric-types swarm the cave.

You can't wait to explore the area! You tie your rope to a nearby tree and climb down the cliff. You're halfway down when a rock slips out from under your feet.

"Whoa-a-a!" you yelp. You grab hold of a tree branch and pull yourself back to the rock. Phew!

"Be careful!" says a tall boy named Flynn down below.

When you reach the bottom, Flynn and his Galvantula greet you. You tell Flynn that you just had a battle with a wild Galvantula that left Blitzle tired.

"No problem," Flynn promises. "You can recharge Blitzle right here with the energy from Chargestone Cave!"

Proceed to **page 16**.